HANS CHRISTIAN ANDERSEN'S

Thumbelina™

THE NOVELIZATION

Adapted by Justine Korman
From a screenplay by Don Bluth
Based on the story by
Hans Christian Andersen

D0596678

Grosset & Dunlap • New York

TM & © 1994 Don Bluth Limited. All rights reserved. Published by
Grosset & Dunlap, Inc., a member of The Putnam & Grosset Group,
New York. Published simultaneously in Canada. GROSSET &
DUNLAP is a trademark of Grosset & Dunlap, Inc. Printed in the
U.S.A. Library of Congress Catalog Card Number: 92-72106
ISBN 0-448-40508-3   A B C D E F G H I J

*Your dreams will fly on magical wings
when you follow your heart!*

Follow your heart and your dreams will fly on magical wings! That's what I always say.

Bonjour! I am Jacquimo—adventurer and lover of romances.

What are romances, you ask? They are stories about people with impossible problems. Samson loved Delilah—that was really impossible! Romeo and Juliet—IMPOSSIBLE! But the most impossible of all romances is impossibly small. Still, I treasure it above all the rest, for I am in the story!

And so I present to you the story of . . . Thumbelina. Now turn the page, and follow your heart!

❀ 1 ❀

Fitting In

Once upon a time there was a kindly woman who had a good farm, a cozy cottage, a healthy horse, a well-tempered cow, a loyal dog, and a coop of lively chickens. In short, she had everything anyone could want. Except for one thing: a child to call her own.

At last the kind woman could bear it no more. So one spring day she paid a visit to a good witch, who gave her a tiny barleycorn.

"Plant this kernel in a flower pot," said the witch. "And see what happens."

The woman did as she was told and by and by the seed grew and grew and grew. Until at last a strange, beautiful bud unfolded on the end of a long, green stem.

"What a pretty flower!" sighed the woman. She kissed the flower and as she did its bright, silken petals opened. In the center sat a teeny-tiny girl of about sixteen years. Her eyes were the deepest blue and her hair was long and golden. She wore a beautiful white gown and a strand of forget-me-nots around her dainty throat.

The woman could hardly believe her eyes. She had

3

a daughter even smaller than her thumb! "I will call you . . . Thumbelina." The mother smiled.

Weeks passed by and the girl grew not an inch. Her mother thought it was strange indeed, but her joy at finally having a child spread over the farm like sunshine.

Everyone on the farm loved Thumbelina, from the smallest mouse to the great, clumsy cows. The faithful dog, Hero, was especially fond of his new mistress. The big, shaggy hound followed her everywhere, and would have gladly given away his best bone to make Thumbelina happy.

And for the most part she was happy. But one small cloud darkened her joy. Thumbelina knew no one else her size. She felt as if the whole world was just too big for her.

Thumbelina tried and tried to fit in. She even tried to help her mother around the farm. But the tiny girl was far too small for chores. She had to struggle to throw one kernel of corn to the chickens—and then had to run away from their scratching yellow feet.

Thumbelina even tried to milk the good-natured cow. But when the cow flicked her tail, she sent Thumbelina sailing into the milk pail with a SPLASH!

The poor little girl could not swim and would have drowned if Hero had not saved her.

After that, Thumbelina just sang.

✿ 2 ✿

Fairy Tales

Every night before bed, Mother read to Thumbelina from a big book of fairy tales.

"Now here's a story about the Noble Dog who saved the king from a wicked wizard," Mother said one evening.

Hero's ears pricked up excitedly.

"Once upon a time," Mother began.

Thumbelina interrupted. "Please, Mother, are there any stories about little people like me?"

Mother thought a moment and turned some pages. "As a matter of fact, there are, Thumbelina. Look."

Thumbelina gazed with wonder at a picture of fairies standing beside a tiny toadstool house. "Oh, my! They *are* little, just like me!" Thumbelina exclaimed. "But what are those things on their backs?"

"Those are wings, my darling. Fairies have wings so they can fly," Mother explained.

"Have you ever seen a fairy?" Thumbelina wondered.

"Well, I thought I did once," replied Mother. Then

she pointed to another page in the book. "Here is a wedding of a fairy prince and princess."

"Do they live happily ever after?" Thumbelina asked, yawning.

"Usually dear," Mother murmured. Then she gently lifted Thumbelina into her polished walnut shell bed.

Thumbelina snuggled down and stroked her tiny chin thoughtfully. "Well, I suppose it works best if two people are the same size?"

Mother nodded. "Yes, of course." She tucked her daughter in between the fresh rose petal sheets.

Thumbelina sighed. "Well, that's not fair. I must be the only little person in the whole wide world. I wish I were big."

Mother said firmly, "Oh, no, Thumbelina. Don't *ever* wish to be anything but what you are. Now go to sleep, my child, and have sweet dreams."

"Mother, would you please leave the book open?" Thumbelina asked. "I want to look at the fairies while I go to sleep."

Mother nodded and propped the book open on a table. Then she kissed her fingertip and touched it gently to Thumbelina's forehead. Mother looked down at Hero. "You take good care of Thumbelina," she said. Then she turned out the light.

As the drowsy dog walked round and round and finally settled in the corner, Thumbelina turned to look at the book in the silvery moonlight.

Thumbelina stared at the prince. He was just her size.

Softly she sang a wish that soon a special someone, like the prince, would find her. Then she wouldn't have to just dream about happy endings. She could live one of her own.

Thumbelina liked that idea so much, she climbed out of bed to dance with the picture of the prince. "I wonder if there really are fairies?" she thought dreamily.

If the tiny girl had only looked outside her window, she would have seen her answer! Just then the fairy queen and king were flying across the moonlit meadow in their rose petal coach, with the royal fairy court following close behind. There were brave knights riding dragonflies and regal maids of honor on snow-white butterflies. A dozen richly garbed trumpeters raised golden reeds in a fairy fanfare.

As she turned to watch the procession, the fairy queen noticed one butterfly had no rider. "Oh my dear," she fussed. "Our son is missing again."

The fairy king looked over his red-robed shoulder. "So he is. I think he feels a bit silly riding that white butterfly we gave him."

"Why should he feel silly?" huffed the queen.

"It doesn't quite make the right impression on the young ladies," the fairy king explained patiently, as he had many times before.

The queen straightened her already straight back. "And what about the impression on the court? Autumn begins today and we must commence the golding of the leaves. Prince Cornelius should be here."

The king groaned.

"I just hope he's not buzzing the vales on that wretched bumblebee," the queen sniffed. "He's the crown prince for heaven's sake. He'll hurt himself," she fretted.

"Dear," replied the king, "have you forgotten what it's like to be sixteen?"

❁ 3 ❁

A Real Prince

Prince Cornelius was indeed riding Buzzbee, his favorite bumblebee—right past Thumbelina's window! When he spied the pretty little girl dancing and singing, the prince buzzed back for a closer look.

"Hello . . . what a beautiful voice. I wonder who she is?" Cornelius muttered to himself. He slipped off the fuzzy bumblebee and whispered, "Stay here, boy. I'll check this out."

With a flutter of his shimmering wings, Cornelius flew silently from the windowsill to the book of tales and hid behind the open page.

Thumbelina ended her dance and sadly addressed her imaginary prince. "Oh, you have to go now? I see. You're a wonderful dancer. Will I ever see you again?"

At this, Cornelius drew his silver sword and slashed through the picture of the toadstool house. He pushed through the page. "May I cut in?" he asked.

Thumbelina stared at the real, live prince. She was instantly charmed by his handsome face and shimmering wings. But she was also startled. So startled that she jumped into a nearby teapot and pulled down the lid. Once safely inside, she studied the prince through a small crack.

"I'm sorry. I didn't mean to frighten you," Cornelius apologized. He dropped his sword. "See? No more sword. Now will you come out?"

Carefully, Thumbelina squeezed out of the spout. She walked slowly around the prince. Her fascinated stare made him uncomfortable.

"Say something, will you?" Cornelius begged.

Thumbelina was almost too stunned to talk. "You're one of them." She pointed at the picture of the fairy wedding.

The prince frowned and pulled himself up to his full height. "I beg your pardon?" he huffed.

"I thought I was the only one my size in the whole world," Thumbelina explained.

Just then, Hero woke up and barked at the tiny stranger. The alarmed prince snatched up his sword and stood before Thumbelina, ready to protect her from the noisy, shaggy giant.

"Hero! No! He's a friend," cried Thumbelina, and she shook the prince's hand to show the dog. "Hello, my name is Thumbelina. How do you do, sir?" she said, smiling. "Thank you for coming to visit."

The prince played along. He bowed and replied, "Oh, no trouble at all. The pleasure is mine."

Deciding that Thumbelina was in no danger, the tired dog let his eyes droop and soon fell fast asleep again.

"Sorry." Thumbelina blushed.

The prince smiled. "Thumbelina! What a lovely name."

The girl blushed again. "Thank you."

"I'm Cornelius," said the prince.

"Cor-nee-lee-us." Thumbelina struggled with the long name, then burst into giggles. "Well, that's a funny name . . . oh, I mean it's perfect."

The prince frowned and an awkward silence fell between them. Then a thought came to Thumbelina's mind. "Tell me about the fairy court!" she blurted. "Is there a . . . prince?"

"Why, yes," Prince Cornelius answered. His eyes twinkled mischievously.

Thumbelina sighed and looked deep into the prince's eyes. "He must be terribly handsome."

"Oh . . . he is," Prince Cornelius said. A playful smile tugged at the corners of his mouth.

"Strong and brave," she continued dreamily.

"None like him," Cornelius declared. Then he took one of Thumbelina's hands in his. The prince had a great urge to kiss this amazing girl.

But Thumbelina chattered on. "I would love to meet the prince."

"I'll tell him," Cornelius promised, and he leaned even closer. But before the prince could kiss Thumbelina, a loud buzzing whirred from the window. "What was that?" Thumbelina cried in alarm.

"That's Buzzbee, my bumblebee. He doesn't like staying in one place too long," the prince explained.

11

Thumbelina giggled and tugged at his hand. "Well, why didn't you say something? Come on."

Gallantly, Prince Cornelius put his arm around Thumbelina's dainty waist and flew her to the windowsill.

"He's amazing!" Thumbelina clapped her hands in delight when she saw the big fuzzy bee.

"Care to go for a spin?" the prince offered.

Thumbelina was confused. "Spin?"

"A flight on his back," explained Cornelius.

Buzzbee flapped his wings eagerly, always ready for an adventure. Skillfully, Prince Cornelius hopped on the bumblebee's back and helped Thumbelina climb up behind him.

"Oh . . . I wish I had wings!" sighed Thumbelina.

"Maybe someday you will," the prince replied. "Now hold tight."

Thumbelina locked her arms around Prince Cornelius's waist. The bee's wings beat faster and faster and Buzzbee took off with a roar! The world dropped away as the bumblebee zoomed across the yard, past the garden wall, and over the grassy meadow.

"Let me be your love. I'll never let you fall. Let me be your wings," Cornelius crooned.

Thumbelina felt as if she had entered a beautiful dream . . . or a fairy tale!

❁ 4 ❁

Forget-me-not

Everywhere they flew, little creatures looked up to admire Thumbelina and Cornelius as they streaked across the starry sky. The heavenly sound of Thumbelina's singing even drifted down to soggy Toad Bog, where Ma Toad was sewing sequins on a ruffly dress.

The flashy toad turned her bulging eyes up from her barge anchored among the lily pads. As she watched the beautiful singer, crafty Ma Toad began to devise a plan.

Thumbelina and Cornelius, however, were blind to anyone but each other as they flew past the bog and over a field of daffodils. The prince showed Thumbelina how, with one touch of his hand, he could make each tender flower burst into bloom.

Yellow petals still danced in the air as Buzzbee circled back to Thumbelina's windowsill. There the tiny couple hopped off the bee, breathless with excitement.

"Oh, Thumbelina, something happened to me tonight . . . something I never want to forget," said the prince.

"Me, too," Thumbelina agreed. Her heart leaped for

joy inside her. Then she lifted the strand of forget-me-nots from around her neck and put them on the prince. "Do not forget me," she said.

Cornelius looked down at the flowers. "I'll never forget you," he vowed. Then the prince took the ring from his own finger and slipped the sparkling blue stone on Thumbelina's hand.

Slowly, Cornelius leaned closer to Thumbelina. But just as he moved to kiss her, the sound of trumpets blasted from the garden below. The fairy court was making its way into Thumbelina's backyard.

"Cornelius!" the queen shouted from the garden.

"Oh, mother," the prince muttered crossly. One kiss, that's all he asked. Sometimes being a prince hardly seemed worth the trouble.

"Cornelius! Come *now!*" the queen commanded.

Quickly the prince took Thumbelina by the waist and flew from the windowsill into her room. "No time to explain." he blurted. "That's the queen of the fairies, my mother . . . ."

"Your mother!" Thumbelina exclaimed.

"Yes . . . now look. I must go now, but can I see you tomorrow?" he asked eagerly.

Thumbelina was too shocked to make much sense. "But . . . a . . . I will . . . your mother?! Then you're the . . . you are . . . tomorrow?"

"Yes, I'm the prince," Cornelius confessed. "Would you like to meet my parents?"

Thumbelina still felt giddy with shock, but managed a nod.

"Cornelius!" the fairy queen called again.

"Oh, say you will!" urged the prince.

"I . . . will," said Thumbelina softly.

Now it was the prince's turn to feel giddy with disbelief. "You will?!"

Thumbelina laughed. "Yes, I will, Prince Cornelius. Oh, yes!"

Then the fairy king's regal voice called out, "Cornelius!"

"I've got to go," the prince said reluctantly.

But Thumbelina could hardly wait until the next day to see the fairy king and queen. She ran to the window to peek out at the garden. "Will they like me?" she worried.

"Yes, they'll love you," Cornelius assured her as he pulled Thumbelina away from the window. "But let me talk to them first. I'll be back for you in the morning."

Thumbelina nodded. "Then you can meet my mother. And then . . . we'll live happily ever after."

The prince smiled and looked into Thumbelina's lovely eyes. "Oh, much longer."

"CORNELIUS!" shouted the King.

"You won't forget to come back, will you?" Thumbelina asked, suddenly afraid that the prince would vanish like a sweet dream in the morning.

But Cornelius smiled and shook his head. "I

promise." Then he jumped on Buzzbee and flew off into the night.

In a delightful daze, Thumbelina drifted back to her walnut shell bed and tucked her tiny legs between the soft petals. Then, her face wreathed in smiles, Thumbelina drifted into her own deep sleep.

So soundly did Thumbelina sleep, in fact, that she did not hear the scraping at her window later that night. Nor did she see the knobby green hands that hoisted Ma Toad up onto the sill. Thumbelina did not even wake when Ma Toad lifted her walnut shell bed and carried it off.

But Hero heard and barked and lunged after the disappearing figures. Furniture clattered to the floor. Toys tipped off their shelves and the book of fairy tales fell flat.

But Hero was too late! He reached the window just in time to see Ma Toad escape with her prize through a hole in the garden wall.

Thumbelina was gone!

❀ 5 ❀

Kidnapped!

The next morning, Mother was stunned to discover Thumbelina's bed missing—and Thumbelina, too! She searched the farm from here to there, but found not a hair of her precious daughter.

The whole farm missed Thumbelina terribly. The cows would not give milk and the chickens were too sad to lay eggs. Their furry and feathered heads all bowed down beside poor Mother's.

"Woof, woof!" Hero barked. "I know what's happened to her."

"Not now, Hero . . . please," Mother scolded. She dabbed at her streaming tears. "My poor Thumbelina. Where, oh, where could she be?"

That is just what the fairy prince wondered also when he arrived later that morning with splendid gifts strapped to his bee. He flew around the room and called for Thumbelina. But there was no answer. Then he noticed Hero dozing in the corner. The prince hovered over Hero's shaggy head and roused him. "Where is she?" Cornelius asked.

"Woof! Woof!" Hero barked. Then he pointed toward the window with his paw.

Prince Cornelius listened intently. "What?"

"Woof! Woof!" Hero pretended to drag something toward the window.

"She was stolen away? Out the window?" Cornelius asked.

"WOOF!" Hero confirmed.

"Who did it?" demanded the prince.

Hero puffed his neck out like a toad, as best he could.

"A toad?" the prince guessed.

"WOOF!"

"Good dog," said Cornelius. Then he bravely drew his silver sword and flew to the window. "I will find her."

"Woof, woof, woof!" Hero was so excited he nearly leaped out the window after the prince. But Cornelius held up his arms. "No, Hero! You stay here and take care of Thumbelina's mother. Let her know everything will be all right." Then the prince jumped on Buzzbee's back, and quick as a wink they zoomed into the air and out of sight.

Not far away, over in Toad Bog, Thumbelina's walnut shell bed rested on a large, soft lily pad. In it lay the little girl, still fast asleep. Ma Toad and her three sons barely blinked their goggly eyes as they watched the tiny girl. Then the morning sun fell over Thumbelina's eyelids and she sat up and stretched.

"Buenos días. I hope you sleep very, very good," Ma Toad said in a thick Spanish accent.

Thumbelina looked around in confusion. Her sleepy eyes widened at the startling sight of Ma Toad and her sons. With her elaborate hair and short, stylish skirt, Ma Toad was rather attractive—for a toad. But her sons were another matter. Each seemed uglier than the last!

"Who are you?" she asked.

"We are the very happy family 'Singers de España.' These are my sons: Mozo, Gringo, and Grundel," Ma Toad said proudly, as if each were a prince. The fat, clumsy toads bowed in turn and grinned.

Then Ma Toad gave Thumbelina a sample of her singing. *"We are very rich and famous."*

Thumbelina became curious. She had never met anyone rich and famous before. "Rich and famous?" she asked.

"Sí! Sí! Mucho," replied Ma Toad. "I bring you here to become famous singer like me!"

But Thumbelina knew that would be impossible. After all, she had to get home! "Oh, no!" she said hastily. "My mother will be very worried." She climbed out of the walnut shell.

Ma Toad shook her head. "Mama no worry. Mama proud when you are a star. She make a big *fiesta* and invite everyone to see her little *niña* who has become big, very, very BIG!"

Thumbelina's eyes widened. "Big? *Big?!*" All her life she had longed to be big.

"And important! Loved by everyone!" Ma Toad bubbled.

"But Cornelius loves me already. I am going to marry him," Thumbelina explained.

Mrs. Toad's thick lips frowned. "Marry him? *Chihuahua!* That would be a very big mistake. It would get in the way of your career in show business. You'd be much too busy washing and scrubbing, cooking and cleaning, and changing diapers."

Thumbelina shuddered. Ma Toad made getting married sound like one awful chore after another.

"Why do that when you can become a big singing star like me?" demanded Ma Toad. "We make big monies together. You make Mama rich. You are important person. You are famous. You are a star!"

Then she and her sons described for Thumbelina the joys of being performers. The bog echoed with their rich, froggy voices while their big flippers slapped against the lily pad.

Thumbelina had to admit she was excited by their glamorous descriptions. What would it be like to sing before a cheering crowd? Was it enough to have one prince love her when she could have whole audiences screaming for more? Thumbelina wasn't sure what to think.

Thumbelina couldn't help herself—soon she was singing along to the Toads' catchy tune.

✿ 6 ✿

All in the Family

Ma Toad wasted no time in preparing her new star. That very same day, Thumbelina sang to a crowd of animals gathered from all over Toad Bog. The audience greeted her sweet voice with wild applause.

While Thumbelina took her bows, Grundel turned to his mother. "Give her to me," he pleaded. "I marry her."

"Very well," agreed Ma Toad. "Then we can keep her in the family. And we can keep the money she earns in the family!"

The applause still echoed in Thumbelina's ears when she finally came off stage. For the first time in her life she didn't feel small. Thumbelina rushed up to Ma Toad. "Thank you! They really like me. Am I a star?"

"Oh, yes—and call me Mama!" Ma Toad added slyly.

Thumbelina looked puzzled. "Mama?"

"Yes! You are going to marry my son, Grundel," Ma Toad explained cheerfully.

"I'm what?" gasped Thumbelina.

"I love Thumbelina," Grundel grunted.

Thumbelina looked at the ugly toad with his silly costume and love in his eyes. Her skin crawled.

"You wait here," Ma Toad instructed. "We'll be right back with the priest!"

"Oh, no, no!" Thumbelina cried. What was happening? "I love Cornelius."

But the toads did not care. They picked up Thumbelina and carried her out to a lily pad far from shore. "Today, you marry my son," Ma Toad declared. Then she swam off to arrange the wedding.

"No! Come back here!" cried Thumbelina. "Wait a second!"

But the toads were gone, leaving Thumbelina alone in the middle of the pond, with no chance of escape. She could not swim!

"Doesn't anybody care what I think?!" cried Thumbelina in frustration. "Help!"

Just then a swallow swooped down through the cat-tails. Seeing Thumbelina was in trouble, he hovered above the tiny girl. *"Bonjour,* little one. Are you having a bad day?"

Thumbelina looked up at the cheerful bird in his colorful vest and feathered cap. His eyes were bright and kind, and Thumbelina liked him right away.

She told him all about how she had met the fairy prince, but was kidnapped by Ma Toad before he could return. "And now Ma Toad says I have to marry her son," Thumbelina concluded.

The swallow cocked his head from side to side. "A toad! That is a very bad day, *Mademoiselle* . . . eh?"

"Thumbelina," she offered.

"Ah, I am Jacquimo. Now how can I be of service to you?" asked the bird.

"Well, I must get off this lily pad," said Thumbelina. "But that's impossible . . . ."

"Ho! Ho! Nothing is impossible," Jacquimo declared. He darted underwater and snipped the lily pad's stem with his sharp beak. *"Voilà!"*

"Oh, my! That was easy," marveled Thumbelina. She started paddling toward the shore. "I just hope I can reach land before those awful toads return!"

But Thumbelina soon realized she was never going to reach the bank. The lily pad was caught in the swirling current of the stream and was rushing toward a steep waterfall!

Jacquimo tugged frantically at the lily pad, struggling to pull it to shore. But the current was too strong. The lily pad whirled closer and closer to the roaring falls. Thumbelina screamed. "Help! Somebody . . . help!" Then she fainted from fright.

Luckily for Thumbelina, two huge bass heard the commotion and swam over to the scene. One fish used his tail to flip the lily pad upstream. The other fish caught the pad on her gleaming back and swam with it to shore.

Other creatures had also heard the cry for help. On the grassy bank, a butterfly grabbed the pad with her feet, while two dragonflies, a ladybug, and one tiny gnat pulled and tugged with all their might. Jacquimo called out encouragement to the kindly insects.

At last, the lily pad was brought safely to rest on the damp grass by the stream. Many pairs of large eyes stared curiously at the unconscious little girl.

"What is it?" they all wondered.

Slowly, Thumbelina sighed and stretched and opened her eyes.

"Look! She's waking up!" cried Baby Bug.

The shy insects darted under leaves and twigs, but Jacquimo stayed by Thumbelina's side.

"Feeling better, little one?" he asked.

"Yes, I think so," said Thumbelina groggily. Then she spied the bugs hiding in the grass. "Who are you?" she asked.

"These are the Jitterbugs," said Jacquimo.

One by one, the Jitterbugs and then the little Jitter-babies came out to meet Thumbelina.

"How do you do?" asked Thumbelina politely.

The Jitterbugs recognized her as the girl they had seen flying across the moonlit field with Cornelius the night before.

"Are you really going to marry the fairy prince?" Baby Bug asked eagerly.

Thumbelina laughed. "Well, if he asks me. He will call for me at my house. That's why I must get home. Besides, Mother will be terribly worried." She sighed. "If only I could find my way home."

"We'll help you!" Baby Bug declared.

One of the dragonflies nodded. "Yeah, nobody'll hurt you."

"Not with us on the job!" the other agreed.

But Thumbelina did not want her new friends to get in trouble on her account. "You'd better not," she warned. "I've got an ugly old toad after me, and he might eat you all up."

"I'm not afraid of toads!" said the first dragonfly defiantly.

"Me neither!" echoed his friend.

"I'll whop him with my tail," said a strong-looking fish.

"I'll sting him," buzzed a bee.

"Oh, you are all very brave. Thank you, but . . . I'm afraid I'll never see my home again." Thumbelina looked down at the lily pad sadly.

But Jacquimo would have none of her moping. "Do you love the prince?" he asked matter-of-factly.

"Yes," said Thumbelina.

"Well, then, follow your heart! It will lead you home. Now . . . where does the prince live?"

Thumbelina thought for a moment. "He lives in the Vale of the Fairies. But I don't know where that is, either."

"Do not worry. I, Jacquimo, will find it and bring *him* home to *you!*" the swallow declared.

"Oh, that's impossible," said Thumbelina.

"Impossible! Nothing is impossible, if you follow

your heart!" cried Jacquimo. "North or south or east or west? Which direction is the best? You don't need a chart. Just trust your heart. Come on, Thumbelina! You're going home! Your mother is waiting."

Jacquimo's rousing speech made Thumbelina feel much better. She kissed the swallow softly on his beak and waved after him as he flapped his wings and rose into the air.

"He's wonderful!" she told the Jitterbugs when Jacquimo was out of sight.

Then, with the Jitterbabies by her side, Thumbelina skipped off down a winding pebbled path. She was on her way home.

❂ 7 ❂

No Joke

Meanwhile, in the magnificent fairy throne room in the heart of the Vale of the Fairies, Prince Cornelius argued with his royal parents.

The queen scolded him. "Cornelius, my sunshine, first you buzz in here on that wretched bumblebee and announce in front of the entire court that you found the girl of your dreams. And now you say she's vanished?!"

"Kidnapped, mother. She's been kidnapped," corrected Cornelius. Why wouldn't his parents listen to him?! Why couldn't they help him?

"You're joking?" was all the queen would say. As far as she was concerned, her son was a hopeless romantic, determined to ignore his royal duties. And the girl wasn't even a princess!

"I wish I were joking," said the prince earnestly. He turned to the king. "Please, Father," he pleaded, "delay the winter frost as long as you can. I need time to find Thumbelina."

Then without waiting for the king's reply, the prince

leaped onto Buzzbee, who stood waiting nearby, and sped away without another word.

Little did Cornelius know that he was also the topic of a heated discussion down on the Toad family barge.

"Pond talk say Thumbelina give you the slip to marry a fairy prince," taunted Gringo. His bulging eyes glowed with pleasure at his older brother's disrupted wedding plans.

Grundel stopped moodily munching flies and looked up. "What fairy prince?" he demanded.

"You no able to show your ugly face on stage no more," Gringo teased.

"Everybody laugh at you," Mozo added.

"*Nobody* laugh!" Grundel shouted back. But his brothers were already clutching their sides, doubled over with cruel laughter. Furious, Grundel grabbed the two by their necks and knocked their heads together.

"I said NOBODY laughs!" Grundel bellowed, and he tossed his brothers overboard with a loud, wet SPLASH. "I go get Thumbelina and bring her back."

In the water, his soggy brothers just laughed harder.

"I marry her!" Grundel declared. And with that he jumped off the barge and hopped off into the night to find the tiny girl.

Thumbelina was, in fact, not very far away. She hummed a happy tune as she continued down the pebbled path under a canopy of twinkling stars. The Jitterbabies, Gnatty, L'il Bee, and Baby Bug, hopped along merrily beside their new friend.

Suddenly, a sly-looking beetle dropped down out of a tree and landed right in front of Thumbelina. The frightened Jitterbabies scattered at the sight of the long-legged beetle with his fancy coat, white gloves, and cane.

"Hi ya, toots!" said the stranger, stroking his curling moustache. "Berkeley Beetle's the name and Razzmatazz is my game. How do you do, how ya feelin'? Everything okay?"

Thumbelina was so surprised she didn't know what to say. "My goodness! Where did *you* come from?" she finally stammered.

Berkeley Beetle pointed to the treetops with his cane. "Up there." Then his beady eyes looked Thumbelina up and down. "I am a connoisseur of sweet nectar, a designer of rare threads, and a judge of beautiful women, and you are *beautiful*, Miss, ah . . . Miss . . . ?"

"Thumbelina, and I'm going home," she said.

But when Thumbelina tried to walk around the beetle, he darted in front of her again.

"What's your hurry, toots? Relax. Take a load off." Berkeley Beetle twitched his moustache in Thumbelina's face.

"I wish you wouldn't do that," she said.

"Perhaps you prefer . . . this!" Berkeley Beetle suggested, as he snatched Thumbelina's hand and planted a kiss.

"Mr. Beetle!" Thumbelina was so embarrassed she giggled. "I don't even know you. Please stop!"

"Stop?" replied Berkeley Beetle. "How can I stop?

I'm crazy about you, toots." He grabbed Thumbelina's other hand and gave it a little kiss. "You're gorgeous," he added, now kissing his own hand. "You're exciting! Delicious!"

Thumbelina was very confused. "I . . . I am?"

Berkeley Beetle pushed his pointy nose into her face. "And . . . I love the sound of your voice," he whispered romantically.

"My voi . . ." began Thumbelina, but Berkeley Beetle interrupted. "Don't talk. Sing! Sing to me."

Then Thumbelina looked up at the tall tree Berkeley Beetle had pointed to. It gave her an idea. "Can you fly me there?" she sang sweetly. Thumbelina pointed up.

"Why should I, toots?" Berkeley Beetle wondered.

"Well . . . from the treetops I could see my house. Then I'd know if I'm traveling in the right direction," Thumbelina explained.

Berkeley Beetle hesitated. "Ah, gee. I don't know. That would be a big, big, very big favor."

"I'll sing for you," Thumbelina offered.

Berkeley Beetle shook his head. "No!" he said as a gleam came into his eyes. "You'll sing at the Beetle Ball." He extended one of his white gloved hands.

Thumbelina held back, but only for a moment. She had to get to the top of the tree. She shook Berkeley Beetle's hand.

"We'll be the talk of the town, toots," Berkeley Beetle said excitedly. Then he grabbed Thumbelina around the waist and with a whir of wings, flew upwards.

30

❈ 8 ❈

That Bug Is a Dog!

Later that night, high in the trees of the Beetlewoods, the Razzmatazz Nightclub bustled and buzzed with beetles of all shapes and sizes dressed in their finest for the gala Beetle Ball.

The band played a fanfare and the velvet curtain rose to reveal Berkeley Beetle and Thumbelina. Even her mother would have barely recognized the tiny girl in her fancy costume. The strange, stiff gown and huge antennae headpiece made Thumbelina look like a big, funny bug.

The audience clapped and cheered for her, and Thumbelina felt the same excitement she had felt when she performed with the toads.

Thumbelina did a little dance while Berkeley Beetle sang. But suddenly her heavy skirt became tangled in her feet. Thumbelina fell flat on her face! Her headpiece tumbled off and her gown fell apart. The music stopped and everyone stared.

As soon as they realized the pretty dancer wasn't a bug

after all, the beetles laughed and jeered. To their beady eyes, Thumbelina was hideous!

"That bug is a dog!" yelled one.

"She's so ugly, she's hurting my feelers!" called out another.

Poor Thumbelina was stung by their rude remarks.

Berkeley Beetle only shrugged. "I'm sorry, toots. I guess you're *too ugly.*"

He flew Thumbelina back down to the ground and sat her gently on a daisy. "Don't worry. You'll get over me," Berkeley Beetle assured her. Then he flew back to join the party, leaving Thumbelina sad and alone. Thumbelina felt as if she didn't have a friend in the world.

But as the lonely girl began to cry, her friends the Jitterbabies were rushing around the Beetlewoods looking for her. When L'il Bee heard her sobs, he called to the others. "Hurry! Thumbelina needs help!"

"Wait for me!" cried Gnatty, who was too little to keep up with the others.

But the tiny bugs didn't get very far before Grundel Toad plopped down out of nowhere and blocked their path. Quickly, the Jitterbabies scrambled under a log. But Grundel followed them to their hiding place and covered the exit with his large, webbed feet. Then he stuck his great, warty head in front of the entrance.

"Did I hear one of you say, 'Thumbelina needs help'?" Grundel growled.

Too frightened to think, Gnatty blurted out an answer. "The beetle took her and flew way up there."

"Gnatty!" scolded L'il Bee. He hurried to clamp his hand over the baby gnat's mouth. He knew it wasn't smart to tell this dangerous toad their business.

"The beetle?" Grundel was puzzled. He didn't understand, but he knew what he wanted. "I want her back!" he croaked.

Grundel quickly lost interest in the Jitterbabies and concentrated on Thumbelina, and when the tiny bugs saw their chance and scurried out of the log, Grundel let them go. He had a different trail to follow. Then he laughed nastily. "Now, we see about this beetle."

All the while, Thumbelina stayed on her daisy-cushion seat, too miserable to move. The sound of someone singing made her finally look up. *"You're sure to do impossible things, if you follow your heart."*

Through her tears, Thumbelina saw Jacquimo fluttering above her. "What's the matter?" asked the swallow.

Thumbelina sobbed. "I'm cold. I'm lost. I'm hungry. And Berkeley Beetle says I'm ugly."

"Do you love Berkeley Beetle?" wondered Jacquimo.

Thumbelina shuddered at the thought. "No!"

"Then never mind the beetle," he said sensibly. "Good riddance to the beetle and good riddance to the toad! Now, does Prince Cornelius think you are ugly?"

Thumbelina straightened up and thought for a moment. She touched the prince's ring, which was still on her finger. "No. He thinks I'm beautiful," she said at last.

"And so you are. Look!" commanded Jacquimo.

Thumbelina gazed into a dewdrop to see a pretty face smiling back at her. Suddenly she felt happy—and also very sleepy.

"I'm going home," she said dreamily, stretching out across the daisy petals. "Jacquimo, will you find the Vale of the Fairies?" she asked as she slowly closed her eyes.

"I promise. But now we sleep," the swallow said with a yawn. *"Bonne nuit.* Goodnight. Tomorrow is a new day and I will go to the forest and find your Prince Cornelius."

"Thank you, Jacquimo," said Thumbelina. Then she drifted off to sleep with the swallow snuggled close beside her.

❂ 9 ❂

On the Trail

Jacquimo set off on his journey early the next morning. The cheerful swallow flew swiftly through the bright, cool countryside, and soon caught up with a desperate-looking rabbit, leaping through grass and twigs.

"Bonjour. Nice sunny day," said Jacquimo.

"It's sunny all right. But I'm not too sure about the 'nice,' " panted the rabbit.

But Jacquimo went on. "I'm looking for the Vale of the Fairies." The swallow didn't notice the hungry fox following close behind the rabbit's cotton tail.

"Fairies, huh? Beats the heck out of me. Why don't you ask a fairy?" the rabbit suggested.

"Oh, you know one?" asked Jacquimo.

"No, but he might." The rabbit nodded in the direction of the tireless fox.

Jacquimo gracefully dropped back—right into the fox's face. *"Excusez-moi, monsieur.* I'm looking for the Vale of the . . ."

"Amskray!" barked the fox.

Jacquimo, however, didn't understand pig Latin and

35

so he did not know the fox had just told him to "scram!" The swallow continued. "I can see you are very busy at the moment, so I'll be brief . . ."

But the fox was through playing games. "Buzz off, buster!" he growled.

Jacquimo was so surprised by the rude fox, he lost his balance and crashed right into a briar bush. Dazed and in pain, Jacquimo examined his wing while the rabbit and fox scampered away. "Oh, no!" he cried. "Look what I've done. I have a thorn in my wing."

Jacquimo tried to shake out the painful briar, but it would not budge. "Oh, *mon Dieu!* This is bad, very bad. I hope I can still fly."

Jacquimo carefully got up to test his wings. To his relief, both worked. "Ah, I fly. Oh, *merci!* And, it only stings a little. Now, where was I?"

Suddenly, red, yellow, and brown leaves poured over Jacquimo. "It's autumn!" he exclaimed. "I must hurry to find the fairy prince."

And off he flew.

Meanwhile, in another part of the forest, above Toad Bog, Prince Cornelius was calling Thumbelina's name, but the whistling wind whipped the words from his mouth. Cornelius clung to Buzzbee's back as the bumblebee struggled to fly through the powerful gusts. Then a leaf struck the prince and knocked him off his saddle. Helplessly, the prince and Buzzbee crashed in a marsh.

Coated with clammy mud, Cornelius dragged himself to drier ground and crawled inside a hollow log which was already crowded with Jitterbugs, also seeking shelter from the storm.

The prince did his best to scrape off the sticky mud. Then he turned to the insects. "I'm looking for a beautiful young woman named Thumbelina," he told them.

"Are you the fairy prince?" asked Baby Bug, noticing Cornelius's glittering wings.

"I am," the prince said.

"Thumbelina's gone," Baby Bug confessed. "Berkeley Beetle took her away."

A large white butterfly pointed outside at the raging storm. "They're out there somewhere."

Prince Cornelius's heart was seized with dread. "She . . . she's out there in that?!" He jumped to his feet and climbed onto Buzzbee. "I've got to find her!"

And they bolted from the log back into the howling wind.

But Grundel Toad was also determined to find Thumbelina, and it didn't take him long to track down Berkeley Beetle. The bug was less than overjoyed to meet the terrible toad.

"I tell you one more time . . . GIVE HER BACK!" Grundel shouted. His large, webbed hands firmly gripped the beetle's scrawny throat.

Berkeley Beetle choked and sputtered. "Okay. Okay. Can I explain something?" he finally stammered.

"What?" Grundel loosened his grip slightly.

"Look. I don't know where she is. We didn't hit it off too well. So I . . . let her go. She's not my type. She's an ugly type. I don't like ugly," Berkeley Beetle spouted in a fearful rush.

POW! Grundel pounded the beetle's head so hard his feet were driven into the ground.

"She is *beautiful!*" the grumpy toad corrected.

Berkeley Beetle's eyes twirled in their sockets. "Whatever you say," he murmured.

POP! Grundel roughly pulled the dazed beetle out of the ground.

"Look, I got an idea," Berkeley Beetle said, coming back to his senses. "I hear that she loves the fairy prince, right?"

Grundel yelled and waved his arms. "I CRUSH fairy prince."

"Okay, okay. Why don't you just nab this prince and set a trap for the girl using him as bait? You know, get her to come to you," Berkeley Beetle suggested.

The slow, rusty wheels began to turn in Grundel's brain. "Nab the prince?"

"Yes! Nab the prince and set a trap!" said Berkeley Beetle. Then he turned and started to leave.

But Grundel wasn't through with his prisoner yet. He lunged and snatched the beetle's wings. "*You* go capture prince."

"My wings . . . You took my wings!" cried Berkeley Beetle. "You can't do that!"

Grundel looked from the wings to the sputtering beetle. "Oh, yeah? I keep the wings until you nab the prince."

"Listen, pal. This harassment has gone far enough and I know my rights. I'll report you to the Pond Patrol," Berkeley Beetle threatened.

Then Grundel grabbed the beetle by the throat.

"Okay. Cool it," choked the beetle.

Grundel released him and Berkeley Beetle gasped. "Where's your sense of humor? All right. I'll nab the prince." Then he called to his friends who were waiting nearby, and together they set off.

✿ 10 ✿

Chills and Spills

Winter came quickly to the countryside, making everyone's journey difficult. Thumbelina shivered each time the bitter wind blasted her with brittle, dead leaves as she trudged through muddy marshes. Finally, the tiny girl spotted an abandoned shoe and crawled inside, exhausted.

Tired and cold, Thumbelina felt her hope fading. "Jacquimo was wrong. I will never find my way home," she declared. "It's impossible. I followed my heart and I'm hopelessly lost."

Her only answer was the howling wind.

But even though Thumbelina was almost ready to give up, her swallow friend flew on despite the thorn still in his wing. He stopped by a cave where a shaggy bear snored loudly in his deep winter sleep.

Jacquimo shouted to be heard above the sound. *"Excusez-moi, Monsieur* Bear. I am looking for the Vale of the Fairies."

The bear mumbled in his sleep. "I don't want no berries."

Jacquimo chirped impatiently. "No, no! Fairies, not

berries. Wake up!" He hopped onto the bear's paw and tugged at his furry ear. But Jacquimo pulled so hard he lost his balance and tumbled beak first into an empty honey pot.

"I said WAKE UP!" shouted Jacquimo from inside the sticky pot.

But the sleeping bear only swatted the honey pot, sending it crashing against a tree outside the cave.

The hard landing didn't help poor Jacquimo's wounded wing. He stumbled out of the pot in so much pain that it took him several minutes to notice how much the weather had changed.

"Winter! Winter is here!" he exclaimed. Just then, a cruel, cold wind lifted Jacquimo off his feet and flipped him high in the air. Jacquimo's wing hurt too much to fly and he somersaulted out of control through the snowy, stormy sky.

In yet another part of the sky, Prince Cornelius continued his search. "Thumbelina! Where are you?" he cried as he and Buzzbee buzzed through the windy weather. Around them, gentle snowflakes had turned to bullets of ice, which froze on the bee's wings. "Don't worry, Buzz. We'll make it," the prince urged as they struggled against the blizzard.

But the gusts were too strong, and suddenly, the prince and his bee were headed straight down. Cornelius crashed into a frozen pond, which cracked beneath his weight. And in no time at all the chill waters had sealed the unlucky prince in a solid block of ice.

41

And that is just where Cornelius was when Berkeley Beetle and his four friends reached the frozen pond.

"If that lousy toad had let me keep my wings, I could have flown after the prince and brought him back in seconds," Berkeley Beetle grumbled. He was so busy complaining, he did not even notice the strange block of ice until one of his friends pointed at it and announced, "Hey, Beetle! This guy's the prince!"

Berkeley Beetle stared in disbelief at the handsome, frozen figure. "The prince!" he finally exclaimed. "Okay, you pick him up. Now let's get out of this stinkin' weather! I can't even feel my feelers anymore."

While Berkeley Beetle griped and groaned, the four other beetles lifted the block of ice and began to carry it down the road . . . right past the snow-covered shoe where Thumbelina lay shivering.

❂ 11 ❂

Three Feet Under

The next morning, the winter sun glistened across a field of stubble poking through a blanket of fresh snow. Near the edge of the field, a miniature stovepipe puffed out a cheery stream of blue smoke. The pipe led underground to a cozy kitchen, where Miss Fieldmouse hummed as she drew a pan of corncakes from the warm oven and stuck a little straw into one to see if it was done.

On a nearby bed, Thumbelina began to stir. Miss Fieldmouse bustled over to her side. "Feeling better, my dear?" she squeaked primly.

"Where . . . where am I?" the girl asked groggily.

"In my kitchen. I'm Miss Fieldmouse, and we are snug and safe underground," replied the mouse.

Thumbelina stared at the mouse in disbelief. "I'm underground?"

"Yes, dearie. Three feet under. I dug it myself with my own two paws," said Miss Fieldmouse proudly. Then she poured Thumbelina a cup of hot tea. "Here, drink this."

Thumbelina took the cup and tried to console herself. "At least the toad won't find me down here."

Miss Fieldmouse regarded her visitor curiously. "You know, there's something I don't understand. Did you really think you could survive the winter in that old shoe? Honestly!" She tittered. This strange little girl was pretty, she thought to herself, but not very sensible!

While the mouse scurried back to her corncakes, Thumbelina looked around the snug burrow for an exit. "I want to go home," she declared.

Miss Fieldmouse shook her pink-bonneted head. "Well, I'm afraid you'll just have to wait here until next spring, Thumbelina."

The girl was surprised. "You know my name?"

"Oh, that was easy. I know much more," the smug mouse said. If there was any gossip flying around, Miss Fieldmouse caught it. "You *were* engaged to the fairy prince, ah . . . Cornelius, I believe?"

"Well, almost," Thumbelina said. Her magical evening with the prince now seemed like a faraway dream.

Miss Fieldmouse clucked her tongue. "How sad that he was found stone-cold frozen in the snow. But, of course, you knew that."

"No! No! No!" Thumbelina cried in disbelief. Her handsome prince could not be gone forever! She flung herself across the bed and began to sob.

Miss Fieldmouse realized her blunder and tried to comfort her guest. "Oh, Thumbelina, forgive me. Sometimes I just blurt things out without thinking. You're still young though. There will be another."

"He was perfect," Thumbelina wept.

"Nobody's perfect," the practical fieldmouse argued. Then she tried to change the subject. "Come along. We'll take these corncakes to Mister Mole. He lives just down the tunnel."

But Thumbelina was too sad to move. "I'd rather not," she said.

"*Well!* I saved your life this very day and you'd rather not?" Miss Fieldmouse huffed.

"Very well," sighed Thumbelina, though all she could think of was her lost prince.

Miss Fieldmouse gathered the hot corncakes in a basket. Then thoughtfully she added, "Oh, one more thing. Is it true you have a beautiful voice?"

The tiny girl wiped more tears from her eyes. "I don't feel much like singing."

"Oh, you must sing for Mister Mole. He loves sweet things. Come on!" urged Miss Fieldmouse.

But Thumbelina was not listening. "Cornelius was looking for me. That's what must have happened," she sobbed to herself as she followed her hostess out of the warm kitchen.

Of course, there were others still looking for Thumbelina. Above ground, Grundel Toad was pacing back and forth and up and down in a gloomy thicket. The toad had worn a knee-deep trench in the earth by the time Berkeley Beetle and his friends arrived with their frozen cargo.

"One ice-cold prince coming up!" called Berkeley Beetle. "Where do you want him?"

Grundel pointed to a pile of compost. "There," he grunted.

The beetles dumped the block of ice.

Then Grundel looked more closely. "He looks dead," he croaked.

"Dead, schmed. What difference does it make? We have a deal, pal. You got your prince, now give me back my wings," demanded Berkeley Beetle.

"You killed him," Grundel whined.

Berkeley Beetle was tired of this toad. "Okay, have it your way. I killed him. Satisfied? Forget the prince, okay? Now, what if I was to tell you I know where Thumbelina is right now, huh? Would you give me my wings?"

Grundel considered, then spoke up. "It's a deal."

"Good. My sources tell me she's buried alive with the mole," the beetle announced.

But Grundel was puzzled. "What mole?"

"If I was you, I'd get my tail over there and save her," Berkeley Beetle advised. "So get hopping and . . . give me my wings, would you please? My wings . . ." Berkeley Beetle snapped his fingers to get Grundel's attention.

The toad, however, was lost in thoughts of Thumbelina. "Where does mole live? I go kick down his door," Grundel croaked angrily. Then suddenly, he grabbed Berkeley Beetle by the arm and started dragging him.

"What's going on? Where are we going?" Berkeley Beetle cried.

"We go rescue Thumbelina from the mole," Grundel rumbled.

Berkeley Beetle fumed. "MOLE! Are you out of your mind? I'm not going down there. Do you know what that guy does to beetles? Do you have any idea?"

"Quiet!" Grundel grunted. He didn't care about moles. He just wanted Thumbelina, and he knew the clever beetle could help him.

"Look, why don't you just go home and marry a toad?" Berkeley Beetle asked. "Did you ever think about that, huh? You find yourself a pretty toad with nice warts and then you marry her!"

But Grundel trudged on, dragging Berkeley Beetle after him.

Neither noticed the tiny Jitterbabies hiding on the other side of the thicket. But the Jitterbabies saw them— and the frozen prince they left behind!

As soon as the villains were out of sight, the Jitterbabies scurried across the thicket, and quick as a wink they built a fire beneath the block of ice that imprisoned the prince.

❂ 12 ❂

Meet Mister Mole

Night was no different from day in the tunnel leading to Mister Mole's house. When at last they reached the end, Miss Fieldmouse knocked briskly on the stately door. Then she fussed with the napkin covering her basket of corncakes.

A servant promptly opened the door and ushered the mouse and Thumbelina into the fancy front hall.

"Good afternoon, Miss Fieldmouse," Mister Mole said in a low, grave voice. He was a squat, slow fellow in a black velvet coat and an old-fashioned collar of stiff ruffles. He leaned on a fancy cane as he waddled over to them on stumpy legs.

"I want you to meet a new friend of mine, Thumbelina," chirped Miss Fieldmouse. "She just came from . . . Up There."

Mister Mole peered at Thumbelina through a pair of thick spectacles which he wore on a chain. "Up There?" He shook his head. "Terrible place."

Thumbelina had to bend back to avoid bumping the

mole's wet, pink nose as he bent over to inspect her. "How do you do, Miss Thumbelina?" he said at last.

"How do you do, Mister Mole?" Thumbelina answered politely.

"Come in, come in!" the old mole commanded. "And don't touch anything. These are *my* things."

The three stepped into Mister Mole's stuffy parlor, and Thumbelina stared in awe at the elegant furniture. Still, the house felt uncomfortably dark and mysterious to her. More than ever, Thumbelina wished she was safe at home with Mother.

"We've brought some corncakes for you. Just you try one, Mister Mole," Miss Fieldmouse offered.

"Oh, hmmmm, yes," the mole agreed, reaching blindly in the wrong direction. Miss Fieldmouse hastily shifted her basket to meet the mole's outstretched claws.

Mister Mole gobbled one corncake, then another, and another. Miss Fieldmouse, meanwhile, daintily poured them each a cup of tea.

"Well, tell us about Up There!" Mister Mole said. "I went up once. Nearly blinded me. Hurried back down fast as I could where it is dark and decent."

"Oh, but I love the light," replied Thumbelina.

"I hate it. End of story!" snapped Mister Mole crossly, cramming another corncake in his mouth.

"Thumbelina, tell Mister Mole a lovely, sad story," Miss Fieldmouse suggested.

Thumbelina didn't really feel like talking, but she seemed to have no choice. "Well . . ." she began.

"Stand right there, where I can see you," Mister Mole ordered, pointing at a stool with his cane.

Thumbelina climbed onto the stool and Mister Mole squinted up at her as she started her story again. "Once upon a time, there was the sun . . ."

"Sing it, Thumbelina. Sing!" Miss Fieldmouse urged.

"She sings?" asked Mister Mole.

Thumbelina nodded and began to sing. As she did, she could see in her mind handsome Prince Cornelius smiling at her as they danced together in the bright sunshine. But then she remembered the prince was gone, and the song ended sadly. *Winter has killed everything . . . even the sun.*

Mister Mole and Miss Fieldmouse clapped as she finished.

"Wonderful story!" cried Miss Fieldmouse.

"Dreadful thing, the sun!" Mister Mole concluded. "And now, I have a story to tell you. During my morning stroll, I stumbled across the most extraordinary thing in my tunnel—a dead bird."

"No!" Miss Fieldmouse exclaimed.

"Yes. I will show you. But how do you suppose a bird got into my tunnel?" the old mole wondered as he tried to show his guests to the door.

Outside, Mister Mole, Miss Fieldmouse, and Thumbelina carried candles as they walked along the mole's dark, cobwebbed Tunnel of Treachery.

"Well, I'm certainly glad I'm not a bird, bothering the world with endless twittering, twittering, twittering," Mister Mole declared.

Suddenly Miss Fieldmouse squeaked. "There it is!"

The three lifted their candles to reveal a bird lying on the tunnel floor. As they came closer, Thumbelina gasped. The bird was Jacquimo!

"Whatever do you suppose happened to him?" Miss Fieldmouse asked, ever eager for gossip.

But Mister Mole didn't care. "Well, there's one less bird to twitter, twitter, twitter Up There," was all he said.

They were both surprised when Thumbelina dropped to her knees to embrace the bird. "Oh, Jacquimo! My dear friend."

Miss Fieldmouse looked from Thumbelina to the mole. "Tender little thing," she remarked.

"Yes, quite lovely," whispered Mister Mole. Then he drew the mouse aside. "Miss Fieldmouse, could I have a word with you?"

"I wish you would," she said cheerfully.

They stepped into the shadows and Mister Mole confided, "You know, I've been meaning to take a wife for some time now."

The gossipy mouse was most interested. "What a lovely idea."

"I find myself, you know, lonely for companionship," explained the old mole. "And I wonder if I could ask you to help me persuade Miss Thumbelina to . . . to . . ."

Mister Mole stuttered, "to be my wife? She could keep me company and sing to me, don't you think?"

"Thumbelina?" asked the mouse, not quite sure if she had heard correctly.

"Yes," Mister Mole assured her. "And for your service in helping to arrange this marriage, I will reward you handsomely!" He handed Miss Fieldmouse a large gold coin.

The mouse hugged the coin to her chest. "Oh, I will! I will! Thumbelina!" she called.

Across the gloomy chamber, the tiny girl sat resting her head on Jacquimo's feathered breast. She did not hear Miss Fieldmouse call. She was listening instead to a . . . heartbeat!

"I can hear your heart!" Thumbelina whispered with joy. "You're not dead at all. No, you're just cold."

"Thumbelina!" Miss Fieldmouse called again.

Thumbelina kissed Jacquimo's closed eyes. "I'll come back tonight," she promised. Then she hurried to join Miss Fieldmouse.

❁ 13 ❁

A Friend in Need

That night in her bedroom, Miss Fieldmouse told Thumbelina about the wonderful match she had arranged for her. "Mister Mole is the richest rodent for miles around. Educated, well dressed, highly thought of! Never mind that he can't see." The mouse giggled. "That's all the better."

Thumbelina could hardly believe her ears. "How could I possibly marry Mister Mole? I don't love him," she declared.

"Love?" inquired Miss Fieldmouse. "Love is what we read about in books, my dear. Marrying for love is foolish. Love won't pay the bills."

Thumbelina stared in amazement at the mouse. Miss Fieldmouse stared right back. To her, life was very simple: warmth in the winter, food in the cupboard, and plenty put aside for a rainy day. What did this silly little girl want with love?

After that, Thumbelina was far too miserable to sleep. She tossed and turned in her bed until she heard Miss Fieldmouse gently snoring. Then she picked up her tiny pillow and blanket and silently made her way back down the mole's Tunnel of Treachery until she reached Jacquimo's still form.

She tenderly placed the pillow under the swallow's head and tucked the warm blanket around him. Then she lay down by his side.

"Please be warm, dear friend. Please live. Poor little swallow. I'm sorry for all the trouble I've caused you." Thumbelina fought back her tears. "I know now, there's no place in this *big* world for *little* people. We cannot do impossible things."

Thumbelina pressed her face into the feathered breast. The tiny girl felt so sad and confused. "Perhaps I should marry the mole," she sighed. Then she thought for a moment. "Yes, I will marry the mole." she declared. "He can take care of me."

Suddenly feathers fluttered and the swallow's faint heart beat faster. "You are joking," moaned Jacquimo softly.

Thumbelina bolted upright in surprise.

"Marry the prince," he continued weakly.

Thumbelina threw herself across Jacquimo's chest and squeezed him in a tight, happy hug. "You're awake! Oh, Jacquimo!"

But the hug hurt the swallow's sore wing. "Ouch!" he cried. "Oh, oh . . . I have a thorn in my wing."

"Oh my goodness!" exclaimed Thumbelina. "Hold still." Carefully she pulled the thorn from Jacquimo's wing, then gently kissed the wound.

Jacquimo laughed. "Ho, ho! Now it will get better." But when he tried to jump to his feet, the bird staggered backwards.

"No. Don't get up," cautioned Thumbelina.

"I go to find the Vale of the Fairies and the prince," Jacquimo argued.

"You silly bird," said Thumbelina.

"Get on my back. I will take you to the green forest," he offered.

"Be realistic," said Thumbelina sadly. "Cornelius is gone."

"I will find him," Jacquimo assured her. Then he sang his familiar song, *"You're sure to do impossible things, if you follow your heart."*

Thumbelina put her hands over her ears so she wouldn't hear his silly, encouraging words. But Thumbelina's friend was determined to help her.

"Bon voyage, mon amie. Follow your heart!" crooned Jacquimo. And with great difficulty, he flapped his way toward a hole in the tunnel ceiling and flew out into the snowy night.

❂ 14 ❂

Wedding March

"Here Comes the Bride" echoed down the underground hall. But Thumbelina did not hear the wedding march or the rustle of her stiff, white gown as its satin train dragged along the dirty tunnel. Nor did she see the crowd of excited guests gathered for the wedding, or the eager look on Mister Mole's round face.

As if in a dream, Thumbelina began to slide the ring Cornelius had given her from her finger. Looking into the shiny blue gem, she could see his handsome face there in the jewel—cold and asleep, never to wake.

She hardly noticed that Reverend Rat had begun to recite the ceremony. "Mister Mole. Do you take this woman to be your lawful, wedded wife?" he asked.

Mister Mole answered grandly, "I do."

The rat turned to the bride. "And, Thumbelina, do you take this mole to be your lawful, wedded husband?"

But Thumbelina heard only Cornelius's voice saying the words he had spoken the night they met. "I'll never forget you."

"Never, never," echoed Thumbelina.

"Speak up!" Reverend Rat twirped impatiently.

Thumbelina slid the prince's ring decidedly back on her finger. "Never," she said aloud.

"I beg your pardon?" sputtered Reverend Rat.

"I cannot marry Mister Mole. I don't love him," Thumbelina explained.

A tremor spread across the room as the guests gasped in horror. Mister Mole stared at his bride, while Miss Fieldmouse shrilled, "Thumbelina!"

Then, to the crowd's further surprise, Grundel Toad leaped forward. "I marry her!" he shouted.

But Thumbelina coolly pushed the toad aside. "No! I won't marry you! I'm going home!" she declared and marched toward the tunnel.

"After her!" commanded Mister Mole.

Berkeley Beetle grabbed her veil. "Hi ya, toots," he chirped.

"I'm not your toots!" Thumbelina said indignantly, unclipping her veil. The beetle tumbled backwards.

Then Thumbelina began to run. Behind her followed Mister Mole, then Grundel, and finally Berkeley Beetle yelling, "Hey! Wait! Wait! My wings!"

At the same time, the Jitterbabies were leading Prince Cornelius into the mole's tunnel. Now thoroughly thawed by the friendly bugs, the fairy prince was determined to find his true love.

Peering over the edge of a steep cliff, Cornelius spotted Mister Mole and his guests chasing Thumbelina across a narrow ledge.

"She marry me!" Grundel was yelling, his webbed feet flapping as fast as they could after them.

The prince flew down into Grundel's path.

The astonished toad could barely speak. "Fairy prince? No!" Grundel grabbed Berkeley Beetle and thumped him. "I thought you killed the prince!"

Cornelius slashed at the toad with his silver sword. "Take that! Come on . . . Show me what you're made of, Toad!"

Grundel seized a flaming torch and swung it wildly. Fearlessly, Cornelius caught the toad by the ankle.

"There! Had enough?" Cornelius demanded. Then he heard Thumbelina cry out in the gloom. And as the prince turned toward the sound, Berkeley Beetle tripped him and Grundel seized his sword. The fight was not over yet!

As for tiny Thumbelina, she was still fighting her own way through the dim, shadowy tunnel. She was too frantic to even notice when she had reached the mole's treasure chamber.

In fact, Thumbelina had almost lost hope when she suddenly glimpsed a shaft of sunlight reflecting off a pile of gold. Looking up, she realized that the sunlight came from a small hole in the ceiling. Using all her might, Thumbelina climbed the steep mound of treasure toward the warm, welcoming light. Then with one final heave, she was free!

✿ 15 ✿

Follow Your Heart

Thumbelina blinked gratefully and stretched her arms to the sun. From above, she heard Jacquimo's familiar voice. *"Always follow your heart."* Then, feathered cap in hand, the gallant swallow was bowing before her.

Thumbelina could not believe her ears when Jacquimo announced that he had found the Vale of the Fairies. "It's true," he assured her. "I talk to the rabbit who talk to the fox, who talk to the bear, who know for sure. I show you. Jump on!" Jacquimo urged.

The swallow lifted Thumbelina onto his back and, before she could object, flew up into the sky.

"This is impossible," protested Thumbelina.

"Ho! Ho! You are wrong," Jacquimo declared.

"I nearly made the biggest mistake of my life," Thumbelina confessed as the swallow winged over the green forest. Then she noticed that the snow had melted and the warm air was sweet with fragrant blossoms.

"I nearly married the mole," Thumbelina went on with a shudder. "But . . ."

"Turn right at the mountain that looks like a turtle," Jacquimo recited to himself.

"But . . . well, I don't love the mole," she continued.

At last, Jacquimo landed in a tangle of ugly weeds. "We are here!" he announced. "Halo-alo-alo! Fairies! This is it."

Thumbelina looked around. How could this ugly place be the Vale of the Fairies? "This just looks like a patch of ordinary weeds," she said.

Jacquimo placed her on a bramble blossom. "Sing, Thumbelina," he chirped.

She looked at him blankly.

"SING!"

And so to humor her dear friend, Thumbelina began softly singing the prince's song. *"You will be my wings. You will be my only love."*

As she did, her voice somehow reached all the way back to the Tunnel of Treachery, where the sweet melody gave Prince Cornelius the strength to beat Grundel and the beetle, despite all their dirty tricks.

But soon Thumbelina stopped singing. "This is silly. These are just weeds. Take me home," she begged. "Please."

But Jacquimo would not let her give up. *"LET ME BE YOUR WINGS!"* he bellowed. "Sing like that."

Thumbelina sighed and gave in. She sang louder and with feeling. It almost made her feel better.

Then she stopped again and faced Jacquimo. "Let's

be practical," she said calmly. "This isn't the Vale of the Fairies, and Cornelius is never coming back."

Thumbelina's song, however, had not ended. In disbelief, she turned. There beside her was the prince finishing the song.

"Cornelius!" she cried.

"Thumbelina," he said, taking her hand. "Will you marry me?"

"I will," she replied in an instant. Her tiny arms flew around him, and finally . . . they kissed!

Magically, the love from their kiss transformed Thumbelina's torn and tattered dress into a beautiful fairy wedding gown. And on her shoulders appeared two tiny fairy wings. Thumbelina found herself giddily drifting off the ground.

"I have my very own wings!" she exclaimed.

Then the brambles they had perched on turned to roses. The whole weed patch, in fact, burst into bloom before them.

In no time at all, heralds were trumpeting the glad tidings of the royal wedding as the fairy king and queen led a procession of hundreds of fairies dressed in their finest. It was all even more magnificent than the picture in Thumbelina's book of tales.

The splendid royal procession made its way through the garden to Thumbelina's farm. Thumbelina and the prince waved to the crowd and blew kisses to Thumbelina's mother, who waved back with tears of joy in her eyes. Hero thumped his shaggy tail and Jacquimo saluted with his mended wing.

Then Cornelius whistled and Buzzbee dove out of the blue sky. And as the fairy prince held Thumbelina securely in his arms, the happy couple flew off at last into the sunshine.

And from that day on, Thumbelina and Cornelius lived happily ever after. *Voilà!*